MADEMOISELLE MOON

First published in 1992 by
Stoddart Publishing Co. Limited
34 Lesmill Road
Toronto, Canada
M3B 2T6

Cover Design: Marie-Louise Gay
Printed in Hong Kong by Book Art, Toronto

Stoddart Publishing gratefully acknowledges the support of the Canada Council, Ontario Arts Council and Ontario Publishing Centre in the development of writing and publishing in Canada.

MADEMOISELLE MOON

Written and Illustrated
by
Marie-Louise Gay

Stoddart

Also by Marie-Louise Gay:

Moonbeam on a Cat's Ear
Rainy Day Magic
Angel and the Polar Bear
Fat Charlie's Circus
Willy Nilly

For Christa

Mister Sun and Mademoiselle Moon
were old friends.
They had known each other
since the dawn of time.
When Mister Sun was born,
Mademoiselle Moon
was there to greet him.
She helped him climb
out of his shell
and they danced the night away...

Flowers grew and waves
splashed high on the moonlit
shores.
Lizards crawled out and smiled
their secret lizard smiles.
Fireflies blinked and dolphins
jumped.
The air smelt of banana cream
and roses. Then Mister Sun
and Mademoiselle Moon went
their separate ways.
Each had a job to do.

For years and years they only
caught glimpses of each other.
Sometimes, on a warm spring
evening, Mademoiselle Moon
would appear, a soft pale face in
the golden sky.
She would wave to Mister Sun
as he slipped behind the
mountains to his bed.

Other times, as Mister Sun emerged in the cool wintry dawn, yawning and shivering, he would see Mademoiselle Moon gliding home after a long night's work.
Like a lovely firefly, she would disappear in a wink between the trees of the forest.
They missed each other a lot.

But one gray, drizzly morning, they met again.
It was Mister Sun's day off.
"Mademoiselle Moon!" cried Mister Sun. "It's been so long! How are you?"
"Not so well," said Mademoiselle Moon. " I feel old and useless. After all these years, I've lost my job! Another moon is starting tonight."
"How terrible!" said Mister Sun. "But still, there are so many things you could do. You could become a doctor or a dancer or... or a pilot or a ..."

"No! No!" cried Mademoiselle Moon. "I don't want to do anything else. All my life I've glided through the sky, shimmered on the sea, and lit up the dark forests. I've rolled the tides in and rolled them out again. I've inspired lovers and poets and... and... O-o-oh, what on earth am I going to do now?"

"Don't you worry," said Mister Sun. "You are my best friend. I will help you."

It had stopped raining and the clouds were gently drifting apart.

"Uh-oh!" said Mister Sun. "It looks like I've got a bit of work to do after all. Wait for me here – I'll be back at dusk."

With that, Mister Sun took a deep breath, dove into the sea, and swam swiftly towards the horizon.

Mademoiselle Moon sighed as she opened her umbrella and sat down to wait and wait and wait.

Hours later, Mademoiselle Moon awoke with a start. "Stars and planets!" she exclaimed. "This is going to be quite a storm!"
There was a tremendous clap of thunder. Lightning forked across the sky and waves pounded the beach. Then Mademoiselle Moon saw the lighthouse. She ran towards it, tugged at the door, and dashed in. It was dark and safe and quiet.

A staircase spiraled up into the darkness. Mademoiselle Moon started climbing. Round and round. Higher and higher. As she neared the top, she heard a voice say,
"Finally! There you are! I've been waiting for you!"
In a shadowy room sat a small fat man warming his feet by a stove.
"Please sit down and have some tea," said the man.

"How could you be waiting for me?" asked Mademoiselle Moon. "I don't even know you."

"I've known you forever," said the man. "I've seen you play hide and seek with the clouds. I've seen you thin as a toenail clipping and fat as a Halloween pumpkin. I'm the lighthouse keeper and... I need your help."

"Me?" said Mademoiselle Moon. "How can I help you?"

"I just can't manage those stairs anymore," said the lighthouse keeper. "And with this storm I know there will be a disaster..." Just then there was a crack of thunder.
KAA-BOOM!

"Please help me..." he said.
"Oh well, I suppose I could
try..." As she climbed the last
set of stairs to the very top,
Mademoiselle Moon grumbled,
"I don't know anything about
lighthouses."
She examined the lantern.
"Just as I thought! I'll never
understand how this works."
There was a tremendous flash
of lightning
and Mademoiselle Moon
caught a glimpse of a
small boat bouncing closer
and closer to the rocks.

"Oh no!" cried Mademoiselle
Moon. "It's going to crash!
What can I do?" She paced
the floor and wrung
her hands in despair.
Then she stopped
and smiled....

Mademoiselle Moon spent the rest of the dark stormy night glowing with happiness. And all the boats came safely back to shore.

At dawn, Mister Sun emerged from the sea, slick and shiny as a seal.

"Mademoiselle Moon! It looks like you found a new job after all!"

"Maybe…" said Mademoiselle Moon, "… and we could see each other every day, couldn't we?"

Mister Sun blushed. The clouds turned bright pink. "You are the lighthouse keeper, aren't you?" asked Mademoiselle Moon.

"I *was*," answered Mister Sun, "but that's *your* job now."